The Thr Billy Goats Gruff

Retold by Annette Smith

Illustrated by Pat Reynolds

NELSON PRICE MILBURN

Once upon a time,
there were
three Billy Goats Gruff.

There was
a little Billy Goat Gruff,
a middle-sized Billy Goat Gruff,
and a great big Billy Goat Gruff.

One day in spring,
the big Billy Goat Gruff said,
"The snow has gone now,
and the grass
on the hillside
is sweet and green."

4

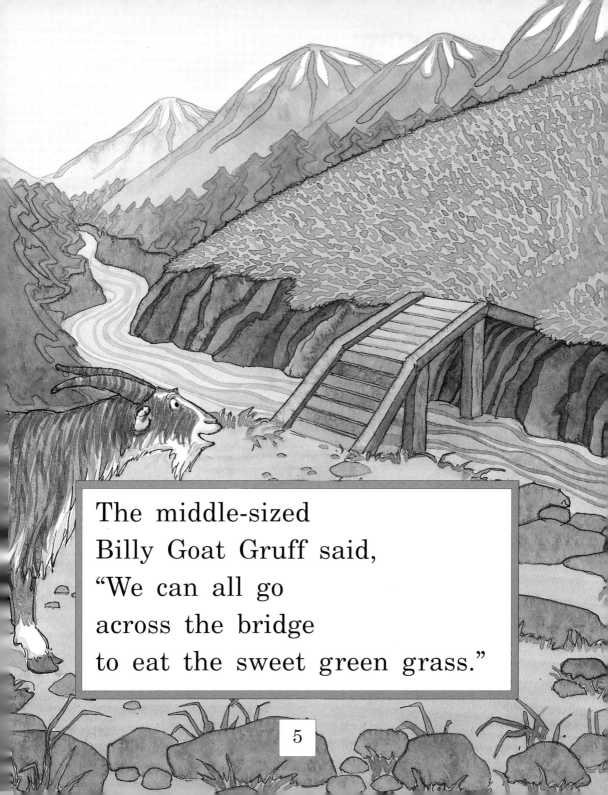

The middle-sized
Billy Goat Gruff said,
"We can all go
across the bridge
to eat the sweet green grass."

The little Billy Goat Gruff
came to the bridge first...

but under that bridge
lived a mean old troll.

Trip-trap Trip-trap Trip-trap

6

"Who's that
coming over **my** bridge?"
roared the troll.

"It's me,"
said the little Billy Goat Gruff.
"I'm going to eat
the sweet green grass
on the hill."

"Oh, no you are not,"
roared the troll.
"I'm coming to **gobble you up**."

"No! No!"
said the little
Billy Goat Gruff.
"Don't eat me! I'm too little.
My big brother is coming soon.
You can eat him!"

"Very well.
Be off with you, then!"
roared the troll.

So the little Billy Goat Gruff
ran over the bridge.

Soon the middle-sized
Billy Goat Gruff
came to the bridge.

Trip-trap Trip-trap Trip-trap

10

"Who's that
coming over **my** bridge?"
roared the troll.

"It's me,"
said the middle-sized
Billy Goat Gruff.
"I'm going to eat
the sweet green grass
on the hill."

"Oh, no you are not!"
roared the troll.
"I'm coming to **gobble you up**."

"No! No!"
said the middle-sized
Billy Goat Gruff.
"Don't eat me! I am too little.
My big brother is coming soon.
You can eat him!"

"Very well.
Be off with you, then!"
roared the troll.

So the middle-sized
Billy Goat Gruff
ran over the bridge.

Then the great big
Billy Goat Gruff
came to the bridge.

Trip-trap Trip-trap Trip-

"Who's that coming over **my** bridge?" roared the troll.

p

"It's **me**!"
said the great big
Billy Goat Gruff.

16

"I'm coming to **gobble you up**,"
roared the troll.

"Oh, no you are **not**!"
shouted the great big
Billy Goat Gruff.

Then the great big
Billy Goat Gruff
put his head down,
and he **ran** at the troll.

He butted him with his horns.
He butted that mean old troll
off the bridge,
and down into the water.

And the three Billy Goats Gruff
never saw
the mean old troll again.

A play
The Three Billy Goats Gruff

People in the play

 Reader

 Big Billy Goat Gruff

 Middle-sized Billy Goat Gruff

 Little Billy Goat Gruff

 Mean Old Troll

Reader

Once upon a time,
there were
three Billy Goats Gruff.
One day in spring
they looked at the grass
up on the hillside.

Big Billy Goat Gruff

The snow has gone now,
and the grass on the hill
is sweet and green.

Middle-sized Billy Goat Gruff

We can all go
across the bridge
to eat the sweet green grass.

Little Billy Goat Gruff

Come on, then.

Reader

So away went
the three Billy Goats Gruff.

The little Billy Goat Gruff
came to the bridge first.

Little Billy Goat Gruff

I'm going over the bridge
to eat the sweet green grass.

(Trip-trap   trip-trap   trip-trap)

Reader

But a mean old troll
lived under that bridge.

Mean old troll *(roaring)*

Who's that coming
over **my** bridge?

Little Billy Goat Gruff

It's me,
the little Billy Goat Gruff.
I'm going to eat
the sweet green grass
on the hill.

Mean old troll

Oh, no you are not.
I'm coming
to **gobble you up**.

Little Billy Goat Gruff

No! No! Don't eat me!
I'm too little.
My big brother is coming soon.
He is bigger than I am.
You can eat him!

Mean old troll

Very well, then.
Be off with you!

Reader

So the little Billy Goat Gruff
ran over the bridge.
Soon,
the middle-sized Billy Goat Gruff
came to the bridge.

Middle-sized Billy Goat Gruff

I'm going over the bridge
to eat the sweet green grass, too.

(Trip-trap   trip-trap   trip-trap)

Reader

The middle-sized Billy Goat Gruff
began to go over the bridge.

Mean old troll *(roaring)*

Who's that coming
over **my** bridge?

Middle-sized Billy Goat Gruff

It's me,
the middle-sized Billy Goat Gruff.
I'm going to eat
the sweet green grass
on the hill.

Mean old troll *(roaring)*

Oh, no you are not!
I'm coming
to **gobble you up**.

Middle-sized Billy Goat Gruff

No! No! Don't eat me.
I am not very big.
My big brother is coming soon.
He is bigger than I am.
You can eat him!

Mean old troll

Very well, then!
Be off with you.

Reader

So the middle-sized
Billy Goat Gruff
ran over the bridge.
Soon the great big Billy Goat Gruff
came to the bridge.

Big Billy Goat Gruff

I'm going over the bridge
to eat the sweet green grass, too.

(Trip-trap   trip-trap   trip-trap)

Reader

The great big Billy Goat Gruff
began to go over the bridge.
But the mean old troll
climbed up onto it, to stop him.

Mean old troll *(roaring)*

Who's that coming
over **my** bridge?

Big Billy Goat Gruff

It's **me**,
the great big Billy Goat Gruff.

Mean old troll

I'm coming
to **gobble you up.**

Big Billy Goat Gruff
Oh, no you are **not**!

Reader
Then the big Billy Goat Gruff
put his head down
and he **ran** at the troll.

Big Billy Goat Gruff
You will not stop me.
I will butt you
with my big horns.
Take **this** and **this** and **this**!

Mean old troll

Ow! Help! Help!

Reader

The great big Billy Goat Gruff
tossed the mean old troll
off the bridge
and down into the water.

Big Billy Goat Gruff

Now, I'm going over the bridge
to eat the sweet green grass
with my brothers.

Reader

And the three Billy Goats Gruff
never saw the mean old troll again.